THE BIG BOOK OF

Animal Crossing

New Horizons

Michael Davis

©2020 CHOUETTE PUBLISHING (1987) INC.

Text: Michael Davis

All screenshots for criticism and review. © 2020 Nintendo. Animal Crossing and Nintendo Switch are trademarks of Nintendo.

CrackBoom! Books is an imprint of Chouette Publishing (1987) INC.

Chouette Publishing would like to thank the Government of Canada and SODEC for their financial support.

Bibliothèque et Archives nationales du Québec and Library and Archives Canada cataloguing in publication

Title: The big book of Animal Crossing: unofficial guide / Michael Davis.

Names: Davis, Michael, 1981- author.

Identifiers: Canadiana 20200082507 | ISBN 9782898022838 (softcover)

Subjects: LCSH: Animal Crossing (Video game)

Classification: LCC GV1469.35.A70 D38 2020 | DDC j794.8/5—dc23

Legal deposit – Bibliothèque et Archives nationales du Québec, 2020.
Legal deposit – Library and Archives Canada, 2020.

TABLE OF CONTENTS

CHAPTER 1

INTRODUCTION

Welcome to the wonderful world of Animal Crossing: New Horizons! This wildly popular life simulation game is in its 5th iteration, meaning that the developers have had many opportunities to learn what players like about the franchise and what mistakes to avoid.

The result is what is widely considered to be the most comprehensive, graphically stunning, and downright fun version of Animal Crossing to date. With hundreds of things to do, thousands of items to collect, and a unique time-gating system, you'll be spending a lot of time on your island.

Purpose

Unlike other types of games that have a clear goal and ending, Animal Crossing is similar to games like Stardew Valley in that there is no way to "win" the game. You can continue coming back to your island day after day without running out of things to do.

That being said, this game does not fall short of goals to achieve, should you care to pursue them. These include:

- Collecting and donating every fish, bug, fossil, and art to the museum
- Completing all levels of every Nook Challenge
- Upgrading every building including your house
- Maximizing your resident occupancy
- Earning a 5-star island rating

All of these long-term goals require a ton of commitment and effort and increase the enjoyment of Animal Crossing.

At the end of the day, it's up to you how you want to spend your time on your island. Whatever you decide, this guide will help you fully understand this game's varied and complex mechanics and offer some useful tips on how to more efficiently achieve your goals.

Interesting features of Animal Crossing

Time-gating

One of the most interesting aspects of this game is its time-gating system. The time of day on your island is determined by your console's internal clock. This means that if you visit your island at midnight, the stars will be out (along with specific bugs, fish, and side events that correspond to that time of day). Likewise, if it's winter in your real life, this will be reflected on your island. Even special holidays like Valentine's Day, Easter, and your birthday are celebrated in the game.

This affects the game in many ways. For example, most building upgrades take a day or two to complete, stores such as the Nook's Cranny have specific operating hours, special events can expire if you miss them, certain fish and bugs only come out at specific

times of day (and even seasons), and some visitors only drop by your island on certain days (for example, Daisy Mae the turnip monger only visits on Sundays before noon).

Each new day in Animal Crossing: New Horizons begins at 5 AM. Although, as we'll cover in the Advanced Tips section, by changing the system clock on your Switch, it doesn't have to!

You can choose whether you want to live in the Northern or Southern Hemisphere at the beginning of the game. This will change the seasonal appearance of some fish and certain time-gated events. For the purposes of this guide, we will be providing information on the Northern Hemisphere.

Customization

At the beginning of the game, you can choose several features for your island. For example, you can pick from a handful of preset layouts, customize the seasons in your hemisphere (North or South), name yourself and your island, and choose your basic appearance. Later on, there will be an almost infinite number of customization options to play around with, but these early choices will affect your island life, so give them some thought.

Economy

Animal Crossing is definitely a game that celebrates capitalism, and many of the features require in-game currency (called Bells) to enjoy. While Bells aren't hard to earn, there are more efficient ways of building up resources, which we'll cover in the Advanced Tips section.

Community

Animal Crossing is more about the journey than the destination. The game's unique features come together to create an experience that will make you want to come back day after day to enjoy the virtual life you've created for yourself. This is why Animal Crossing has built up such an impressive fan base. You can easily enjoy engaging with online communities to share your progress and show off your island.

CHAPTER 2

BASIC THINGS TO DO

Without enemies or bosses to fight, what exactly can you do in Animal Crossing? You'd be surprised at just how much.

Catching bugs

Bugs can be kept and put in storage or on display in your house. However, you'll most likely want to sell them to Timmy Nook at the Nook's Cranny, or Flick, an island visitor who pays 1.5 times the basic shop price for bugs.

Bugs can also be kept and put on display around the island. The first time you catch a bug, consider donating it to Blathers at the museum where it will be added to an exhibit that you can visit.

The Critterpedia on your phone keeps track of all of the bugs you've caught, interesting facts about them, and how many new bugs you have left to discover.

Catching fish

Fish can also be found in most bodies of water in and around your island. When caught, new species can be donated to the museum or sold either in the Nook's Cranny or to C.J., a fishing enthusiast who will periodically visit your island.

New fish are documented in the Critterpedia, along with basic information such as what habitat they prefer, as well as the best time of day and time of year to find them. In the Tools section, we will outline some strategies for finding rarer fish to complete your collection or sell for lots of Bells.

Just like bugs, fish can also be displayed in your house or around the island and can even be gifted to other island residents!

Digging up fossils

At least 4 new fossils can be found around your island every day. They are marked by a star on the ground where the grass has split and the soil is peeking through. Fossils can be assessed and identified by Blathers at the museum, and then donated if he doesn't already have one in his

collection. Otherwise, they can be sold for Bells or put on display in your house or around the island.

Collecting resources

There are many different types of resources to collect in Animal Crossing, such as:

- Fruits
- Turnips
- Flowers
- Weeds
- Sticks

- Stones
- Iron Nuggets
- Clay
- Regular Wood
- Softwood

- Hardwood
- Star Fragments
- Bells
- Gold Nuggets

These resources can be sold or used in DIY recipes to create new items. Just like in real life, some resources, like gold and iron nuggets, are more valuable than others. Specific information on each type of resource is included in the Resources section.

Selling items

A great way to earn Bells is to sell items from your inventory to Timmy Nook, who runs the Nook's Cranny. But don't forget that there are other island visitors that might be interested in purchasing specific items such as fish, bugs, or plants at a higher price than the general store.

Buying items and DIY recipes

There are a staggering number of items to buy in this game—from furniture to clothing, customization kits and tools, and even music albums! Many of these items can be categorized as "cosmetic" items (clothing, handbags, and furniture) or "utility" items (tools, travel tickets, and DIY recipes for upgrades).

Customizing your items, house, and island

While not all customization options are immediately unlocked, you will eventually have the ability to customize patterns on clothing, your phone case, the terrain, and even your island flag!

While these changes are largely cosmetic, part of the fun of this game is making your island as unique as you are!

Crafting DIY recipes

Once learned, a DIY recipe becomes available to craft on any workbench, provided that you have the required resources. Some recipes, just like most tools, require you to craft a lower-quality version of them before you can craft the next quality level.

Donating to the museum

Once the museum is built, you'll be able to donate three types of finds to its halls: fossils, fish, and bugs. If you donate 60 species, the museum will expand to add a wing to display donated art.

CHAPTER 3

TOOLS

Tools are important for collecting resources, getting around, and even staying dry in Animal Crossing New Horizon. Each tool serves a different purpose, some more useful than others.

Breakable vs. non-breakable tools

While tools such as the Pole, the Ladder, the Ocarina, and the Umbrella last forever, most tools used to harvest resources have a limited number of uses before they break (and you need to buy or build a new one). There are three levels of tool durability.

Flimsy

Flimsy tools are the least durable and will only last a limited number of uses before breaking and disappearing.

Regular

Regular tools are sturdier and last longer than flimsy tools.

Golden

Golden tools are unlocked by achieving specific goals—they have the highest durability level. The specific requirements to acquire DIY recipes for golden items are different for each tool and will be covered in their respective sections.

Golden tools are not indestructible and require a rare and valuable gold nugget for each crafting session. So, it's worth considering hanging onto your gold to craft rare furniture.

Alternate tools

Alternate tools are additional versions of the regular tool with cosmetic differences but the same durability.

Customizing tools

As the game progresses, you can customize the color of your tools using a Customization Kit at a DIY workbench (which is gifted to you fairly early on in the game by Tom Nook). Don't worry if you've lost or sold your Customization Kits, you can always buy more at the Nook's Cranny for 600 Bells.

Customizing your tools allows you to change their color and reset their wear and tear to zero. This can come in handy if you get sick of crafting or buying new tools when they break or want to make sure that a rare golden tool doesn't break from overuse. It's much easier to periodically change the color of your tool to reset its value!

The Tool Ring

The Tool Ring can be purchased at the Nook Stop for 800 Nook Miles. It creates a handy shortcut that allows you to equip tools by pressing up on the directional pad. Once there, you can navigate to your tools using the left joystick and then pressing "A" when the desired tool is highlighted.

You can customize which tools are featured on the Tool Ring by opening up your inventory, pressing "A" when the item is highlighted, choosing "favorite," and then assigning a slot for them on the Tool Ring.

There are more tools than there are slots on the Tool Ring, so give some thought as to which ones you'll need most. Frequently used tools that definitely deserve a spot on the Tool Ring are your fishing rod, shovel, stone axe, pole, ladder, slingshot, and net.

Let's take a look at some of the tools, their durability stats, and how to most effectively use them!

Stone Axe and Metal Axe

Overview

The axe is an essential tool that allows you to collect resources such as wood and stone, as well as cut down trees, and destroy rocks (when your strength is boosted by eating fruit).

Axe durability varies by type, but you will lose 1 durability point when you:

- Hit a rock (regardless of whether it produces an item)
- Hit a tree or bamboo shoot
- Destroy a rock with fruit boost

Axes do not lose durability when you:

- Swing the axe and don't hit anything
- Hit objects that are not rocks or trees
- Hit other villagers or visiting players

Types of axes

There are two types of axes in Animal Crossing, the Stone Axe and the Metal Axe. The major difference between them is that the Metal Axe is capable of chopping down trees after three hits, whereas the Stone Axe cannot.

Most of the time you'll find yourself using the Stone Axe, as you may not want to risk cutting down a tree. However, sometimes you may want to chop down the odd tree, as the stump left behind can attract special bugs. If you find that the stump is an eyesore, you can always dig it up with a shovel.

Both the Stone and the Metal Axe come in several types.

Flimsy Axe – 40 durability

You will be awarded the DIY recipe for the Flimsy Axe after you give Tom Nook 2 fish and/or 2 bugs at the beginning of the game. This recipe requires 5 sticks and 1 stone.

Stone/Metal Regular Axe – 100 durability

Once you have the recipe for the Flimsy Axe, you can buy a recipe book from Timmy Nook called the "Better Tools Guide," to get the recipe for a Regular Axe. This recipe requires 1 Flimsy Axe as one of its ingredients, along with 3 pieces of wood and either 1 iron nugget for the Metal Axe or 1 stone for the Stone Axe.

Stone/Metal Golden Axe – 200 durability

You will be given the recipe for the Golden Axe DIY after you destroy (use up) 100 Flimsy Axes, Stone Axes, or Metal Axes. To reach this goal faster, consider using Flimsy Axes for most of your resource collecting, as their durability is lower, and they wear out faster.

The Golden Axe recipe requires 1 Regular Axe and 1 gold nugget.

Using the axe

Collect wood/fruit

Each tree can be chopped three times and will drop one of the three types of wood for every swing. Again, be careful with the Metal Axe as the third chop will bring the whole tree down. If you chop a tree with fruit on it, the fruit will drop after the first chop, but you can still keep swinging to

receive three pieces of wood.

Mine rock

Like the shovel, the axe can be used to chip off pieces of rock. Be careful not to hit the rock with a Metal Axe after you've eaten some fruit or else you'll destroy it. Rocks are a very valuable renewable resource on your island that won't come back immediately after you destroy them.

Cut down trees

Only the Metal Axe is capable of cutting down trees, and once they're cut down, they won't grow back—make sure that you want them destroyed. That being said, stumps attract specific types of bugs which can be handy.

Shovel

Overview

The shovel is an extremely useful tool for collecting various resources and digging things up around your island.

Shovel durability varies by type, but you will lose one durability point every time you:

- Hit a rock
- Successfully dig up a buried object (such as a fossil)
- Dig up vegetation such as saplings, flowers, weeds, etc.
- Dig up a rock or tree after eating fruit to boost your strength

Actions that do not affect shovel durability are:

- Hitting any object that isn't a rock (such as a tree)
- Digging an empty hole
- Filling in holes
- Planting items (such as flowers or saplings)

Types of shovels

Flimsy Shovel – 40 durability

You will receive the DIY recipe for the Flimsy Shovel as a gift from Blathers, the museum curator.

To get one, you must:

- Trigger the building of the museum by donating 5 unique bugs and/or fish to Tom Nook
- Choose a spot for the museum
- Wait an in-game day
- Talk to Blathers, the museum curator, and receive the DIY recipe for the Flimsy Shovel
- Craft a Flimsy Shovel using 5 pieces of hardwood

Regular Shovel – 100 durability

The Regular Shovel can be crafted using the DIY recipe found in the "Better Tools Guide" recipe book that you can buy from the Nook Stop. Crafting one requires 1 Flimsy Shovel and 1 iron nugget.

Alternate Shovels – 100 durability

Alternate Shovels have the same stats as the Regular Shovel (100 uses)—they just look different. They include the Colorful Shovel, the Outdoorsy Shovel, and the Printed-Design Shovel.

Golden Shovel – 200 durability

You will receive the recipe for the Golden Shovel when you help Gulliver find the parts for his Communicator 30 times (see the Special Events section for more information on Gulliver). Crafting one requires 1 Regular Shovel and 1 gold nugget.

Using the shovel

Digging up fossils

At least 4 new fossils can be found around your island every day (marked by a star shape on the ground where the grass has split and the soil is peeking through). The shovel is handy for digging them up. Fossils can be kept, sold, or assessed and donated to the museum.

Mining rock

While you can also use an axe to mine rocks, you can whack your shovel against rocks to yield resources such as stone, iron, gold, clay, and even Bells!

Each rock can yield up to 8 resources, enough to surround the rock. However, the amount is based on the time you spend mining, so the longer you take, the fewer resources you get.

Since each rock hit recoils your character backwards slightly, and you lose time by moving closer to the rock again, a good tip is to dig two holes behind you and stand between the holes and the rock when hitting it. This will allow you to keep pressing "A" as quickly as possible so that you get all 8 items.

Digging up flowers and trees

See a flower you like? You can dig it up and plant it somewhere else! You can even dig up trees, although you'll have to eat fruit to supercharge your strength beforehand.

Finding buried Bells

When you dig up a patch of earth that is glowing gold, you will find Bells. You can also bury more Bells in the hole to create a money tree that will grow bags of Bells instead of fruit. See the Advanced Tips section to learn more.

Mission items

In some temporary quests, you may be required to dig. A good example of this is the Gulliver quest, which requires you to dig up lost pieces of his Communicator in the sand.

Clams

You may see wisps floating out of patches of sand on the beach. These are Manila Clams which you can dig up and use to craft the DIY recipe for fish bait.

Fishing rod

Overview

Fishing is a fun activity that allows you to discover and collect new types of fish to donate to the museum, decorate your house/island, and complete your Critterpedia. You can also sell them to Timmy Nook at the Nook's Cranny or wait for a visit from C.J. so that you can sell them for a higher price or have him make you a model.

Fishing rods lose durability when you:

- Successfully catch a fish, garbage, or eggs

Fishing rods do not lose durability when you:

- Cast the rod
- Reel in the line without catching anything
- Fail to cast the rod

Types of fishing rods

Flimsy Fishing Rod – 8 durability

The Flimsy Fishing Rod recipe is included in Tom Nook's DIY workshop, or you can buy one off of Timmy Nook for 400 Bells. Crafting one requires 5 tree branches.

Regular Fishing Rod – 30 durability

The Regular Fishing Rod recipe is unlocked when you buy the "Better Tools Guide" recipe book. Crafting one requires 1 Flimsy Fishing Rod and 1 iron nugget.

Alternate Fishing Rods – 30 durability

Alternate Fishing Rods include the Colorful Fishing Rod and the Outdoorsy Fishing Rod.

Golden Fishing Rod – 90 durability

The Golden Fishing Rod recipe is awarded when you catch every fish in the Critterpedia. Crafting one requires 1 Regular Fishing Rod and 1 gold nugget.

Using the fishing rod

Different fish come out at different times of day, so if you're interested in catching as many different fish as you can, switch up the time and place of where you fish. For example, some fish only live in the sea, while others might be more at home in a pond or river. Some feed at all times of day, while others prefer the morning and early evening.

Scaring fish

Some fish get spooked if you run up to them too quickly, so always approach slowly.

Fish direction

When fishing, aim your cast to be as close to the front of the fish as you can (the front is the rounded part of their shadow). Depending on the fish, your lure can be further away from them than you might think, but they will never engage with a lure that is behind them.

When to reel

Once a fish has noticed your lure, they will often nibble before they bite. A nibble makes a subtle water rippling sound, and the lure doesn't move much in the water. If you press "A" to reel in your line during one of those nibbles, the fish will get away.

Wait for a bite—this is indicated by a louder splashing noise and a more pronounced movement of the lure. If you press "A" when you feel a bite, you'll reel in the fish with no problem.

If you find that you are accidentally reeling in too soon, try closing your eyes and listening for the sound of a bite. The nibble and bite sounds are so different that eliminating visual cues may help you focus on just the right sound. With this strategy, you should never regret losing the "one that got away" ever again. Fish will not nibble more than 4 times without biting.

Fish bait

Fish bait can be used to force a fish to spawn. Fish bait can be bought at the Nook's Cranny or crafted using a DIY recipe that contains a Manila Clam (found by digging on the beach where you see wisps of sand floating out of the ground).

Fish bait will not increase the chances of catching a rare fish, but you can target specific places such as ponds, rivers, or off the end of piers to make sure that you are targeting the right fish habitat.

Watering can

Overview

The watering can allows you to water your plants to make them grow faster and is useful for growing hybrids (see the Advanced Tips section to learn more about hybrids). The Flimsy Watering Can is only able to water one plant at a time. When you upgrade to the Regular Watering Can, each time you water, the drip swings back and forth to cover 6 squares in a 2x3 radius.

Watering cans lose durability when you:

- Water flowers that have not been watered yet (you lose 1 durability point regardless of how many flowers are hit with water)
- Water grass with no plants (you lose $1/20^{th}$ of a durability point each time)

Watering cans do not lose durability when you:

- Rewater plants that you've already watered in the same day (resets each day)

Types of watering cans

Flimsy Watering Can: Waters 1 square – 20 durability

Once you donate 4 bugs and/or fish to Tom Nook, he will reward you with the DIY recipe for the Flimsy Watering Can. Crafting one requires 5 pieces of softwood. This version of the tool can only water one space at a time.

Regular Watering Can: Waters a 2x3 square area – 60 durability

The Regular Watering Can covers a larger area—a 2x3 square area in front of you. The DIY recipe for this tool becomes available when you buy the "Better Tools Guide" recipe book from the Nook Stop. Crafting the Regular Watering Can requires 1 Flimsy Watering Can and 1 iron nugget.

Alternate Watering Cans: Waters a 2x3 square area – 60 durability

Alternate Watering Cans have the same stats as the Regular Watering Can—they just look different. They include the Colorful Watering Can, the Outdoorsy Watering Can, and the Elephant Watering Can.

Golden Watering Can: Waters a 3x3 square area – 180 durability

This is a difficult DIY tool recipe to acquire. You must achieve a 5-star rating for your island before it unlocks. For tips on how to achieve this rating, check out the Advanced Tips section. Once you receive the recipe, it will cost you 1 Regular Watering Can and 1 gold nugget to craft.

While the golden version of most tools simply increases their durability, the Golden Watering Can expands its coverage to a 3x3 space and can turn black roses into golden roses by watering them.

Using the watering can

There's not much to using the watering can. You can water flowers once a day, although you only need to water the ones that are wilting if it hasn't rained in a while. You can tell that flowers have been watered because they sparkle. Watering flowers also speeds up the process of creating hybrid flowers, which is discussed in more detail in the Advanced Tips section.

Net

Overview

You use the net for catching bugs, wisps (see the Special Events section for more information) and cherry blossoms. Since there are 80 types of bugs to collect and donate to the museum, keep an eye out for them!

Nets lose durability when you:

• Catch anything

Nets do not lose durability when you:

• Swing the net and don't catch anything

Types of nets

Flimsy Net – 10 durability

Tom Nook gives you the DIY recipe for the Flimsy Net right around the time he gives you the DIY recipe for the Flimsy Fishing Rod. It requires 5 sticks to craft.

Regular Net – 30 durability

You will be given the DIY recipe for the Regular Net when you buy the "Better Tools Guide" recipe book. Crafting one requires 1 Flimsy Net and 1 iron nugget.

Alternate Nets – 30 durability

Alternate Nets have the same stats as the Regular Net—they just look different. These include the Colorful Net, the Outdoorsy Net, and the Star Net.

Golden Net – 90 durability

You will unlock the DIY recipe for the Golden Net when you catch all 80 bugs at least once. Crafting one requires 1 gold nugget and 1 Regular Net.

Using the net

The net can reach 2 squares in front of your character and is swung in whatever direction you are facing. Holding down the "A" button allows you to creep slowly with the net, which is handy for bugs that spook easily, such as bees, moths, and tarantulas.

The net can be used to catch flying bugs such as butterflies and dragonflies, as well as bugs that move along the ground (or even on water like the diving beetle) such as beetles and hermit crabs. See the Phone section for tips on catching hard-to-find bugs.

Slingshot

Overview

The slingshot's only purpose is for shooting down balloons that float over the island. But this is important, as balloons award presents such as Bells and DIY recipes.

Slingshots only lose durability when you successfully bring down a balloon. Otherwise, you can fire rocks into the sky to your heart's content.

Types of slingshots

Regular Slingshot – 20 durability

You can buy the DIY recipe for the Regular Slingshot from Timmy Nook for 300 Bells or buy the slingshot itself for 900. We recommend that you craft your own slingshot since the required 5 pieces of hardwood shouldn't take you much time to collect.

Alternate Slingshots – 20 durability

Alternate Slingshots have the same stats as the Regular Slingshot—they just look different. Alternate slingshots include the Colorful Slingshot and the Outdoorsy Slingshot.

Golden Slingshot – 60 durability

The DIY recipe for the Golden Slingshot is unlocked after you shoot down 300 balloons. After this goal is complete, a golden balloon will drift over the island, and when shot down, will yield the DIY recipe for the Golden Slingshot. From there, you'll need 1 Regular Slingshot and 1 gold nugget to craft it.

Using the slingshot

Shooting down balloons can be a bit of trial and error in terms of where to stand underneath. Line your character up horizontally with the balloon and watch the rock that is shot from the slingshot to see whether it goes behind or in front of the floating present. If behind, move down for your next shot, if in front, move up. You can also use the right analog stick to change the camera perspective slightly if that helps you line up your shot.

Ladder

Overview

The ladder allows you to reach elevated areas of your island. Later on, you will be able to build ramps to save time, but in the early stages of the game, the ladder is very useful for getting around. It does not break, no matter how many times you use it.

Types of ladders

There is only one type of ladder in Animal Crossing: New Horizons. To get one, you must first help Timmy build the Nook's Cranny Store, unlock Blathers' Museum, and invite a new resident to your island (you sometimes meet potential new residents while using Nook Miles Tickets to explore other islands).

After the new resident as been on your island for a day, speak to Tom Nook and he will give you the DIY recipe for the Bridge Construction Kit. Build the bridge, pick out a plot for the incoming villager, and finally, Tom Nook will send the ladder DIY recipe to you through your phone.

Crafting the ladder requires 4 pieces of regular wood, 4 pieces of hardwood, and 4 pieces of softwood.

Using the Ladder

Simply equip the ladder and press "A" when you are near an elevated area—you'll be able to climb right up! Conversely, when you come to a drop-off, press "A" to climb down.

The ladder is a key tool for making the daily rounds on your island, as elevated areas often have buried fossils.

Pole

Overview

The pole allows you to cross narrow rivers, which is essential for exploring parts of your island early on in the game. Later on, you'll be able to build bridges, but the pole is always a handy tool for getting around.

Types of poles

There is only one type of pole, and it can never break. You will receive the DIY recipe for the pole from Blathers at the Museum once it opens for business, so don't delay in getting that museum open!

Using the pole

Press "A" near the edge of a river to cross it. Some rivers may be too wide to cross, so if it isn't working, walk down the riverbank until you find a narrower spot.

Magic wand

Overview

The magic wand is a tool that allows you to rapidly switch from 8 preselected outfits without visiting your wardrobe. Kind of like a Tool Ring but for clothes! Wands can never break.

Types of wands

Star Wand

To unlock the DIY recipe for the Star Wand, you must chat with Celeste, who will appear in the evening somewhere around your 20th day of playing the game. The recipe requires 3 Star Fragments and 1 Large Star Fragment, which you can collect during a meteor shower (see the Event section for more details).

Alternate Wands

You can acquire DIY recipes for Alternate Wands that look different. The recipes are often earned by participating in special events, and include:

- Bamboo Wand
- Bug Wand
- Bunny Day Wand
- Cherry-Blossom Wand
- Cosmos Wand
- Golden Wand
- Fish Wand
- Hyacinth Wand
- Ice Wand
- Iron Wand
- Lily Wand
- Mums Wand
- Mushroom Wand
- Pansy Wand
- Rose Wand
- Tree-Branch Wand
- Tulip Wand
- Wedding Wand
- Windflower Wand

Using the magic wand

Once you have the magic wand, you will have the option to design preset outfits when standing at your wardrobe. After that, when you are out and about, pressing "A" while holding the wand will open a radial menu, which you can then use to select any of the preset outfits that you like!

Umbrella

While technically the umbrella is a tool to keep you dry, it doesn't really have any effect on gameplay. It is more decorative than anything. Different types of umbrellas are often for sale in the Nook's Cranny. If you see one that you like, buy it, because it might not be there tomorrow!

Ocarina

The ocarina is also a cosmetic tool, although it's fun to play. Try rapidly pressing "A" to create a randomly generated melody. You can also draw out notes by holding down the

"A" button. So, while you can't compose a proper song, you can have some fun making music.

The ocarina never wears out. The recipe for the ocarina can be bought as part of the DIY for beginner's recipe book (which costs 480 Bells) from Timmy Nook. After that, you can craft it by using 5 pieces of clay.

CHAPTER 4

YOUR PHONE

If you thought escaping to an isolated tropical island meant leaving the trappings of civilization behind, you were wrong! In this game, you have a trusty smartphone, which has many useful features.

Camera

Your in-game phone can take photos, zoom in and out, and apply filters. Pictures taken in-game can be shared from your Switch's picture app to social media platforms such as Twitter and Facebook or exported via microSD card.

If you just want to take a quick photo, simply press the capture button on your Switch controller (the white square button below the directional pad).

Nook Miles

This section of your phone allows you to check your Nook Miles balance and receive rewards for completed challenges. The main menu lists long-term goals such as catching

500 fish. Press the + button to access randomized Nook Miles Challenges that are easier to complete, like selling 5,000 Bells' worth of goods, or collecting 10 pieces of wood.

When you complete a Nook Miles Challenge, an icon will appear on your screen in the top left corner along with a sound cue to let you know that you have some Nook Miles to collect. Collect your Nook Miles as soon as you can, because a new challenge will appear that you may have been planning on completing anyway.

DIY recipes

This screen allows you to see which DIY recipes you've collected and whether or not you currently have the resources that you need to craft them. You'll need a workbench to craft any recipes, but knowing that you're only a couple of pieces of wood short can save you the hassle of going to a workbench when you're missing some resources.

Custom designs

This app allows you to draw and create your own custom patterns and designs to apply as skins to your furniture and clothing—and after Isabelle is unlocked, even your island map.

Critterpedia

This app organizes which bugs and fish you've found, along with information about the species, such as their preferred habitat, and at what time of day and time of year you can catch them. An empty square means that you haven't yet discovered the specific bug or fish for that slot yet.

Bugs

There are 80 bugs to catch. See all of them in Appendix A at the end of this guide. While many bugs are easy to spot and catch, here are some that are more notable than others.

Tarantulas and scorpions

Tarantulas and scorpions are bugs that fight back! But they're worth catching—after you donate one to the museum, you can sell them for 8,000 Bells!

To catch a tarantula, hold down the "A" button with your net to sneak up closer. When it rears on its hind legs, stop, then move closer once it settles down. With a little patience, you'll catch it!

Wasps

Wasp stings will swell up your face something fierce. The swelling will go down with medicine that you can buy from the Nook's Cranny or craft on a workbench. However, you can wait and the swelling will naturally go away the following day.

Wasp nests drop from some trees when shaken and can be caught if you're quick. While shaking trees, have your net equipped, and after the nests drop, run away a few squares, then turn around and press "A" to catch them with your net. If you get the timing right, you'll avoid a nasty sting and add a new bug to your Critter-pedia!

Mole crickets

Mole crickets are active from November to May and are identified by the loud buzzing noise that they make. When you hear it, crank up the volume and experiment with moving around to see when the noise gets louder. When the noise is at its loudest, try digging around with your shovel. A mole cricket will pop out and you must quickly switch to your net to catch it. You'll have to move fast as they can fly away and you'll have to start all over again.

Fleas

Fleas only appear between April and November in the Northern Hemisphere and between October and May in the Southern Hemisphere. Villagers may become infested and complain of itchiness, so just hit them with the net to cure their problem and add a flea to your bug collection.

Ants

Ants appear near rotten turnips on the ground. All you have to do is buy turnips on a Sunday before noon and then leave them on the ground for a week until they rot the following Sunday.

Flies

Flies are drawn to rotten turnips and trash, so leave some lying around to attract these guys.

Fish

There are also 80 fish to catch. See all of them in Appendix B at the end of this guide. Your ability to catch a fish will depend on their preferred:

- Habitat (sea, rivers, ponds)
- Time of day
- Time of year

Because of this, it's almost impossible to catch all 80 types of fish in under a year, because you must wait for each season to come around for all of the different fish to appear. Some fish are rare and can be sold for big money.

Football Fish (5,000 Bells)

This fish is one of the more common rare fish and appears in the sea between November and March from 4 PM to 9 AM.

Sharks (8,000 to 15,000 Bells)

Sharks are one of the few fish you can identify from their silhouette because they have a small fin. There are 4 types of sharks that can be caught throughout the year. Whale Sharks and Hammerhead Sharks can be caught any time of day, and Great White Sharks and Saw Sharks can only be caught from 4 PM to 9 PM.

Oarfish (9,000 Bells)

This massive fish has an extra long silhouette and can be found in the sea between December and May at any time of day.

Blue Marlin (10,000 Bells)

This fish can be found from November to April and from July to September at any time of day. It can only be caught by heading to one of the piers on your island—using fish bait will increase your odds of catching it.

Golden Trout (15,000 Bells)

This fish is found in elevated rivers at the highest point on your island between March to May and September to November between 4 PM and 9 AM. This is a very rare fish, so you can work the odds in your favor by bringing a bunch of fish bait and forcing spawns at specific spots. Then all you can do is cross your fingers and hope for the best!

Coelacanth (15,000 Bells)

This is one of the rarest fish across all Animal Crossing games! It only appears when it's raining, but otherwise can be found in the sea all year round at any time of day.

Map

You probably won't need to consult your map much, as the basic layout of your island is pretty simple. However, if you get lost, the map shows landmarks such as major buildings and the location of your fellow island residents and temporary visitors in case you want to talk to someone specifically.

Rescue Service

If you need to return to your house, you can use this feature to teleport. That being said, this service costs Nook Miles, which can be put to better use buying furniture, clothing, and DIY recipes. So, it's worth trying to find your way back on your own.

Call Islander

This app is unlocked later in the game and allows you to enter multiplayer mode. You can enter either with 4 players on the same console (called couch co-op) or with 8 other players online (unlocked during day 2) if you have a Nintendo Switch Online subscription.

You can team up with your friends and explore an island together. One player is designated the leader and the others are followers. Only the leader can craft DIY recipes and talk to villagers.

Island Designer

The Island Designer app gets unlocked well into the game after you receive a visit from K.K. Slider (see the K.K. Slider section for more details).

The Island Designer allows you to make major changes to your island, including redoing its basic layout and changing terrain by adding ramps and bridges (which must first be bought at the Resident Services Building). However, you do need to buy permits to get to work, which you can buy at the Nook Stop. The permits are:

- Waterscaping Permit: 6,000 Miles
- Cliff Construction Permit: 6,000 Miles
- Arched Tile Path Permit: 2,000 Miles
- Dark Dirt Path Permit: 2,000 Miles
- Sand Path Permit: 2,000 Miles
- Stone Path Permit: 2,000 Miles
- Terra-Cotta Tile Permit: 2,000 Miles
- Wooden Path Permit: 2,000 Miles
- Custom Design Path Permit: 2,300 Miles

Passport

The Passport is a handy summary of your player character. You can customize your photo, title (new ones are unlocked by completing Nook Mile challenges), and a short bio on your profile so that people who view it can get to know you a little better.

Best Friend List

The first time you play online, you will unlock the Best Friend List. This allows you to send best friend requests to players you have interacted with online. Playing multiplayer with best friends unlocks the shovel and the axe, which are otherwise not permitted when you play with regular friends.

The app also lets you chat with your best friends and keeps a log of conversations.

Nook Shopping app

After you buy 100 items at the Nook Stop, you are given the Nook Shopping app that allows you to browse the catalog on the go. You can only buy 5 things a day as they are sent to your mailbox.

CHAPTER 5

INVENTORY

Your inventory is how many items you can hold at any given time. You start out with 20 slots, which is not a lot considering that several of those slots are occupied by necessary tools. You can add 10 slots by buying an upgrade from the Nook Stop for 5,000 Nook Miles.

Another 10 slots are unlocked after the 3rd new resident arrives on your island and you help Tom Nook get him settled. Check the Nook Stop for the next upgrade which will give you a total of 40 slots for an additional 8,000 Nook Miles.

Expanding your inventory is one of the best investments you can make in the game, as even with 40 slots you'll always be wishing you had more space to carry resources.

CHAPTER 6

RESOURCES

Just like in real life, there are multiple types of resources that have value in Animal Crossing New Horizon.

Bells

Bells are the basic currency on your island and are depicted as gold coins. These can be used to upgrade your house, purchase DIY recipes, flowers, saplings, clothing, tools, furniture items, and much more.

Bells are not difficult to earn, but there are more efficient strategies to generate revenue, which will be covered in the Advanced Tips section.

Nook Miles

Think of these as reward points. Nook Miles can be exchanged for items (and even Bells if you buy a Bell Voucher and cash it in at the Nook's Cranny).

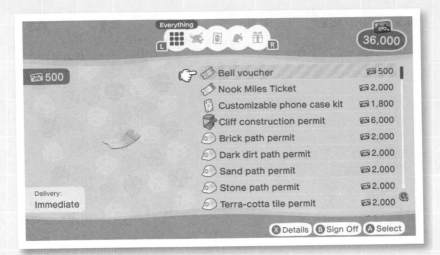

Nook Miles are not awarded for buying or selling things, but for unlocking achievements and claiming them through the Nook Miles app on your phone.

They are worth collecting because they can score you unique items, as well as valuable Nook Miles Tickets which allow you to go on Mystery Island Tours and gather more Bells and resources.

Along with the 83 Nook Miles Rewards categories, there are also daily Nook Miles Challenges that multiply Nook Miles earned by 2 or 5. These challenges are randomly generated and are replaced once you claim them, so claim them as soon as you complete one, as it may be replaced with a task you were about to do anyway. May as well get some rewards!

There are different regular Nook Miles Rewards you can earn in the game. Most of them have 5 objectives, some have less, some have more. For every objective you complete, you get a few hundred Miles, and it can even go up to a few thousand.

Basic materials

A major part of Animal Crossing is the various DIY recipes that allow you to build your own furniture, tools, and clothing. However, each recipe calls for its own specific building materials.

Stones

Stones are the most common material mined from rocks and are used in many recipes, most notably the Stone Axe.

Tree branches

Branches can be found on the ground near trees or may fall out of any trees that you shake. If a tree drops a branch, you can shake the same tree numerous times to drop more branches. This can be handy if you're hunting for branches but don't want to risk a hornet's nest falling out from shaking several different trees.

Weeds

Weeds are used in a small number of DIY recipes and are also slow to grow back, so maybe don't weed your whole island at once. Weeds can be useful for earning Nook Miles, as a regular multiplier challenge involves selling 20 clumps of weeds. Also, Lief, an occasional visitor to the island, loves buying weeds and will offer you 20 Bells per clump of weeds.

Wood

There are three types of wood:

- Regular wood (yellow with dark brown bark)
- Hardwood (dark brown)
- Softwood (yellow)

Wood is harvested with either the Stone or Metal Axe, and each tree generates three types of wood. The tree will reset at the beginning of a new day. Wood is a valuable material for making DIY recipes and can be sold at the Nook's Cranny.

Clay

Clay is harvested from hitting rocks with a shovel or an axe and can be used to make some DIY recipes, most notably the ocarina.

Bamboo

Bamboo is harvested from bamboo trees, which are not native to your island, so keep an eye out for them when you go on Mystery Island Tours. Make sure to dig up a bamboo tree with your shovel by eating fruit and then bring it back to your island.

Young spring bamboo

This is another type of resource that can be harvested from bamboo. Think of it as bamboo's equivalent of softwood.

Junk

Sometimes when you're fishing you might pull up an old tire, a used boot, or even a can. These items can be used in a limited number of DIY recipes or to attract flies. However, they will not be accepted as gifts by the other island residents.

Gold nuggets

Gold nuggets are extremely rare and can be sold for Bells. However, we recommend that you save them to craft golden tools once you have the recipes.

Iron

Iron is found by hitting rocks with a shovel or an axe, although it is much less common to find than stones or clay. Early on in the game, iron is needed to move forward, so make sure that you don't sell it. Since rocks are limited on the island and can only be mined once a day, you don't want to get caught without iron. Another option: use Nook Miles to purchase airline tickets to visit a randomly generated island and harvest iron from rocks you will find there.

Plants

Picking plants

Plants can be picked by simply pressing "Y" when next to them to collect the flowers (for use in DIY recipes and decoration). They can also be uprooted using the shovel and transplanted to other places. This goes for full-sized trees as well, however, you will need to eat some fruit before attempting to dig them up.

Moving plants

You can easily dig up a flower using the shovel. Stay on the lookout for new flower types when visiting other islands, by checking the sales at the Nook's Cranny, or by looking at what Lief has on offer.

Growing plants

You can also grow your own flowers and trees by buying seeds and planting them in the ground. Flowers tend to grow after 3-5 days if watered once a day.

Hybrid flowers

You can create your own hybrid flowers by taking the two plants that you want to cross-breed and planting them one square apart (leave one blank square in between). Eventually, the plants will fill in the empty space with a hybrid flower type that you can't find anywhere else.

An easy way to do this is to designate a 5x5 square space and create a checkerboard pattern. Start with the first plant, then leave an empty space, then the second plant, an empty space, then the third plant. In the next row, start with an empty space, then the first plant, then an empty space, then the second plant, then an empty space. This way, you are giving your plants the best opportunity to create hybrids. You can make the grid as big as you like, and place fences between hybrid projects so that there is no accidental cross-pollination. Don't run through your flowers as it wrecks their petals!

Shells

Shells can be sold or used in some DIY recipes. This is not a great resource to sell, since the purchase prices are relatively low, and they take up a lot of space in your inventory. However, as they spawn quite frequently, they are a reliable source of Bells.

Shell Name	Price	Shell Name	Price
Pearl Oyster	1,200 Bells	Oyster Shell	450 Bells
Giant Clam	900 Bells	Venus Comb	300 Bells
Conch	700 Bells	Sea Snail	180 Bells
Scallop Shell	600 Bells	Sand Dollar	160 Bells
Coral	500 Bells	Cowries	60 Bells
White Scallop	450 Bells	Porceletta	30 Bells

Star Fragments

Both Regular Star Fragments and Large Star Fragments do not occur regularly and can only be collected during a meteor shower. See the Special Events section for more information on acquiring Star Fragments.

Balloons

Balloons spawn every 5 minutes out at sea, and then slowly float to shore. You can use the slingshot to shoot them down and receive a gift. There are two types of balloons. Red balloons drop Bells and blue balloons drop DIY recipes.

A good strategy for finding balloons is to set a 5-minute timer while you're playing. Once the timer goes off, run up and down your beaches to catch the balloon as it reaches the shore. Balloons are a great way to find recipes you might never otherwise get a chance to collect.

Fruit/nuts/wasp nests

There are several types of fruits and vegetables that you can collect in this game. However, only one type grows natively on your island (randomly picked at the start of the game). They are:

- Oranges
- Apples
- Cherries
- Coconuts (coconut trees can only be planted on beaches)
- Pears
- Peaches
- Acorns (only available in the fall)
- Pinecones (only available in the fall)
- Wasp nests (randomly fall out of some trees)
- Cherry Blossom Petals (caught with a net in spring)

Don't worry, you can always transplant a tree from another island so that you can grow all types. It's worth your while because fruits that are not native to your island sell for a higher price!

The best way to expand your fruit collection is to visit other islands. You can either do this randomly by buying Nook Miles Tickets and visiting randomly-generated islands or coordinating with your friends to see if they have the types of fruit trees that you are looking for.

Selling fruits is a great source of income, but they can also be eaten to supercharge your character. Eating fruits allows you to perform feats of strength, such as digging up entire trees or destroying rocks (not recommended as they are a valuable renewable resource and in limited supply). If you have ever eaten fruit and wanted to turn off the supercharge effect, you can actually relieve yourself in the bathroom (if you have crafted one) to reset your strength.

Turnips

Turnips are different from fruits because they can't naturally be collected on the island. They can only be bought from Daisy Mae in bundles of 10 on Sundays before noon. Once the Nook's Cranny has been upgraded to become a standalone store outside of Tom Nook's building, you can check in every day to see what turnips are selling for— usually somewhere between 90 and 110 Bells per bundle of ten. You can buy as many turnips as you like, providing you have enough Bells.

In this sense, the turnip market is kind of like a mini stock market (it's even is nicknamed the Stalk Market). Buying them at a low price and waiting for them to become overvalued could mean big money.

If you don't sell your turnips before the following Sunday, they rot and lose their value. However, letting them rot on the ground attracts unique bugs such as ants and flies.

Turnips can't be stored in your house storage, but you can toss them on the floor if you want to free up inventory space. Turnips that are left outside can be picked up by visitors, so make sure to fence them in to make sure that they stay in your possession.

You cannot sell turnips on Sundays. The Nook's Cranny changes its buy prices for turnips twice a day, at 5 AM and again at noon. A decent buying price for turnips is 200 Bells for a bundle of 10, however, the price can be as high as 600 Bells.

CHAPTER 7

BUYING AND SELLING

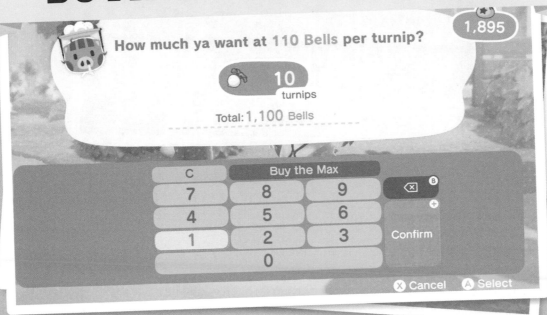

While Animal Crossing is quite the island paradise, it is definitely not a commune. There is a healthy economy at work, which you quickly realize when Tom Nook gives you your hefty moving-in bill! But don't worry, it's pretty easy to make money (or "Bells"), and it's a lot of fun saving up for the perfect items to decorate your house, upgrade your living space, and even change the terrain of your island.

There are several spots on the island to buy and sell items and keep that Animal Crossing economy moving.

Nook Stop

While the Resident Services Tent (which eventually becomes a brick and mortar building) has many other features that are outlined in the Building section, a major part of it is the Nook Stop. This is a kind of mail-order service where you can exchange Bells or Nook Miles for items, recipes, and upgrades.

You can only buy 5 items per day at the Nook Stop, and physical items will be delivered to the mailbox outside of your house the next day. Things like recipes and Nook Miles Tickets can be printed out and received immediately.

After you make 100 purchases at the Nook Stop, you will unlock an app that allows you to buy items directly from your phone. However, it's still a good idea to log in to the terminal every day because you earn more Nook Miles for each consecutive day you log in—up to 300 Nook Miles a day. Not bad for something that takes less than 10 seconds!

The Nook Stop inventory changes every day, so if you see an item that you want, you better make a move or you might miss your chance.

At this terminal, you can also use Bells to buy a rotating stock of furniture and clothing items, deposit money into a savings account (which earns a small amount of interest on your capital), and pay off any debts you have built up with Tom Nook.

The Nook's Cranny

Timmy, the owner of the Nook's Cranny starts off by mooching off Tom in the Resident Services Tent. After you upgrade your house, he decides to strike out on his own and asks that you help him find basic materials to help him build a standalone store. This is worth your while because it greatly increases the number of items you can buy and unlocks several other aspects of the game.

To help upgrade the Nook's Cranny, you'll have to donate:

- 30 pieces of regular wood
- 30 pieces of softwood
- 30 pieces of hardwood
- 30 iron nuggets

Wood is relatively plentiful on your island, but with limited rocks to mine, and each of those rocks paying out a low amount of iron nuggets, they will be your toughest resource to find. If you are feeling impatient, you may want to purchase a Nook Miles Ticket and take a Mystery Island Tour. You'll probably find several new rocks to mine so that you don't have to wait for yours to reset.

The new store will have a wider variety of items to buy, and a rotating display of fun items that you can buy and put in your house. If you see something you like, don't delay in buying it because it probably won't be there tomorrow!

You can also sell items, including the "hot item of the day," which is an item that Timmy will pay about double the regular price for. In practice, there are much more efficient ways to make money, but sometimes Nook + challenges require selling a hot item, so it can be worth your while.

Finally, you can check the buy prices for turnips and sell any in your inventory that you bought from Daisy Mae to Timmy on Sundays between 5 AM and noon. The price of turnips changes twice a day, at 5 AM and at noon, so wait for the right price, and check out the resources section for more tips on playing the Stalk Market.

The store hours are from 8 AM to 10 PM but don't despair if you want to unload items outside of operating hours. You can put anything that you want to sell in the drop box outside the store, and the payment will be sent to your mailbox the following day. However, you won't be able to take advantage of hot items or bonuses outside of store hours.

The Able Sisters tailor shop

Before you can build the tailor shop, you must first complete the following tasks:

- Help build the museum (donate 5 bugs and/or fish to Tom Nook and an additional 15 to Blathers)
- Upgrade the Nook's Cranny (donate 30 units of all types of wood and 30 iron nuggets)
- Wait for Mabel to appear in the Resident Services Plaza selling clothing

- Spend around 5,000 Bells in her store to convince her it's a good idea to set up shop
- Help her find a suitable location
- Wait until the next day

The tailor shop is much like the Nook's Cranny, but exclusively for clothing. Here you will find a large selection of clothes that you can try on in the shop before buying.

Other visitors

Not every visitor to the island sets up a store. Many of them wander the island or set up a cart in the town square. Always take advantage of their visits because they come at random intervals, bring unique items to sell, and will also sometimes buy resources from you at a premium.

Saharah (interior design)

Saharah sells floors and wallpaper for your house. She also offers "mysterious" versions of these things which are randomized items that you can't choose.

C.J. (fish enthusiast)

C.J. appears randomly on your island, but also on every second Saturday of the month for an official fishing tournament. For more information on fishing tournaments, see the Special Events section of this guide.

You can interact with C.J. in three different ways:

Buying fish

C.J. will buy fish for 1.5 times what they offer at the Nook's Cranny.

Fishing challenges

C.J. may challenge you (e.g. catch 5 fish in a row or 3 fish of the same size) and then buy the fish you caught afterward.

Fish models

C.J. will create fish models for you, free of charge. If you give him 3 of the same type of fish he will mail the model to you. These models can be used to decorate your house.

Daisy Mae (turnip sales)

Every Sunday from 5 AM to noon, Daisy May will appear in the village square and sell turnips. These can be sold any day other than Sunday at the Nook's Cranny, which offers fluctuating buy prices that change twice a day at noon and midnight. Daisy's turnips cannot be stored in your house and will spoil if not sold within a week.

Flick (bug enthusiast)

Flick makes random appearances on the island and unlike Blathers, the museum curator, he LOVES bugs! Flick hosts the Bug Off, which occurs on the 3rd Saturday of every month during the summer. Additionally, Flick offers two services:

Buying bugs

Flick is happy to offer 1.5 times the price the Nook's Cranny offers for any bugs you want to unload. This might not sound like much but considering that a tarantula regularly sells for 8,000 Bells, it's worth your while to save them for his visits.

Bug models

If you bring 3 bugs of the same type to Flick, he will create a snazzy model for you.

Celeste

Celeste is Blathers' sister and she loves the stars. She randomly appears about 20 days into the game after sunset. If you speak to her, she'll inform you that wishing on shooting stars can bring good luck (it actually gets you Star Fragments, which is explained in more detail in the Events section). Celeste will also give you the DIY recipe for a Star Wand.

Leif

Leif appears on random days and sets up shop in the town square. Leif sells flowers and plants that you might not be able to find at the Nook's Cranny. He also (for some reason) loves weeds and buys them from you at 1.5 times the regular price. It's a good idea to hang onto your weeds until Leif appears, as otherwise they don't fetch much of a price.

K.K. Slider

K.K. Slider is one cool dog, and you might have seen his name in the Nook Stop where you can buy his albums. He will not appear in your village until you have unlocked the Resident Services Building and helped Tom Nook build housing plots and a campsite plot. After that, he'll hem and haw about how K.K. is too cool to visit the island unless you earn a 3-star rating (see the Advanced Tips section for strategies on getting a 5-star island rating). Once you do, K.K. will come to visit every Saturday. You can request songs from him so that you can collect tunes that aren't available in the store.

Once K.K. visits and plays his first song (the game's welcome song), you will unlock the ability to terraform your island.

At 6 PM on Saturdays, he'll take requests for specific songs, or you can ask him to pick one randomly to play. He'll also show up on your birthday (or whatever birthday you specified at the beginning of the game) and play a special tune for you.

Kicks

Kicks sells shoes and bags and randomly appears in the Resident Services Plaza, so keep an eye out for him. Once you've bought a unique item from Kicks, it will be available to buy from the Nook Shopping terminal or app.

Label

Label is unlocked after the Able Sisters tailor shop is open for business. She appears on random days in the Resident Services Plaza.

Label is all about holding fashion contests and rewards players for wearing clothes that match her theme. Don't worry if you don't have the right clothes, Label will give you some to wear. Simply change into the outfit and talk to her again to receive a prize.

Redd (art and furniture dealer)

Redd is a shifty art dealer that nevertheless is a fun and interesting character. He is unlocked after you upgrade your museum and donate at least 60 items. After that, Redd will show up and demand the exorbitant price of 498,000 Bells (!) for a piece of art. Don't worry, he'll come down to the more reasonable number of 4,980 Bells for your first purchase.

The art and statues you buy from Redd can be donated to the museum or sold. But beware of fakes, which cannot be donated or sold—but do look pretty nice on your wall!

Redd's ship pulls up to the small beach on the north side of your island, so it's worth checking for him every day. You can avoid walking all the way up there by looking at your map. If he's there, he will show up on the map.

When it comes to Redd's counterfeit art and statues, buy wisely because you can only purchase one piece of art per day. Use the following guide to decide what you should buy.

Art that is always real

- Warm Painting
- Calm Painting
- Flowery Painting
- Moody Painting
- Dynamic Painting
- Worthy Painting
- Glowing Painting
- Common Painting
- Sinking Painting
- Nice Painting
- Proper Painting
- Mysterious Painting
- Twinkling Painting
- Perfect Painting
- Great Statue
- Familiar Statue

Art that is potentially fake

Study the real painting by searching online so that you can spot minor differences between the real and fake. Beware, the following paintings and statues may be fake!

Paintings:

- Serene Painting
- Wistful Painting
- Academic Painting
- Graceful Painting
- Jolly Painting
- Famous Painting
- Scary Painting
- Scenic Painting
- Moving Painting
- Amazing Painting
- Quaint Painting
- Solemn Painting
- Basic Painting
- Wild Painting Left Half
- Wild Painting Right Half
- Detailed Painting

Statues:

- Warrior Statue
- Motherly Statue
- Beautiful Statue
- Robust Statue
- Gallant Statue
- Informative Statue
- Ancient Statue
- Tremendous Statue
- Mystic Statue
- Rock-Head Statue
- Valiant Statue

CHAPTER 8

OTHER MAJOR BUILDINGS

Your house

The first decision regarding your house is where to put it. It's largely a matter of personal preference, but we recommend you build your house on the main island. It isn't until later in the game that building bridges to cross rivers becomes an option, so for the sake of convenience, it's a good idea to be on the same landmass as your neighbors, as well as the village square and general store. Don't worry, you can always move it later for a fee.

The tent you start out with is fairly modest and small, with storage space to hold 40 items. None of this really matters, as you can easily leave items on the ground and they won't go anywhere. However, customizing the interior of your house and your yard is an extremely fun and varied task—there are a ton of decorative items to buy and craft.

Storage

Inside the house, you can press right on the directional pad to open up your storage and retrieve items. To store an item, simply press "X" to open your inventory, then press "A" when the item you want to store is highlighted. Finally, navigate to "Put in storage" and then press "A" again.

Decoration

There are two ways to arrange furniture and decorations in your house. You can walk to where you want to place it, open up your inventory, press "A" on the item and then select "Place Here."

Once items have been set down, you can slide them around by holding down "A" and moving in the direction you want them to go.

You can also press down on the directional pad to open up a more robust decorating system that allows you to specifically place and rotate items using a top-down view.

Outside of your house is a mailbox, where you receive mail-order packages, messages, and gifts from friends you've met on the island or through online play.

Upgrading your house

At first, your house is just a tent and even that comes with a debt to Tom Nook of 5,000 Bells. Once you pay that off, you can talk to him and receive a loan to upgrade to a house. You can't upgrade your house until any outstanding debt has been paid off.

There are a lot of upgrades—upgrading your house to the maximum will set you back 5.696 million Bells.

The possible upgrades include:

- Tent-to-house upgrade (98,000 Bells for 6x6 squares, one room, 80 storage slots)
- House size upgrade (198,000 Bells for 8x8 squares, one room, 120 storage slots)
- Backroom (348,000 Bells for a second room, 6x6 squares, 240 storage slots)
- Left room (548,000 Bells for a third room, 6x6 squares, 360 storage slots, unlocks the ability to customize your mailbox and roof going forward)
- Right room (758,000 Bells for a fourth room, 6x6 squares, 400 storage slots, unlocks the ability to customize doors)
- Second floor (1,248,000 Bells for a second floor, 10x6 squares, 800 storage slots, unlocks the ability to customize your house's siding)
- Basement (2,498,000 Bells for a basement, 10x6 squares, 1,600 storage slots)

Resident Services

Resident Services starts out as a simple tent in the lower-middle of your island and houses both Tom Nook and Timmy Nook's fledgling general store. Here you will find:

- A DIY workbench that you can use for crafting (free of charge)
- The Nook Stop, a terminal that acts as a bank account as well as a shopping kiosk for buying items

- Access to Timmy's general store (which eventually turns into its own building called the Nook's Cranny later in the game)
- A storage bin with occasional free low-value items randomized at the beginning of each day

The Resident Services Building eventually has two staff members.

Tom Nook

Chats with Tom Nook open up options to upgrade your house (for a fee), celebrate the opening of new buildings, take DIY crafting workshops, get advice, and later on, purchase island infrastructure such as ramps and bridges.

Tom is a major character early on in the game, and the one to talk to when you want to expand your house, learn new recipes, and even donate bugs and fish before the museum is opened.

Tom also loves to organize ceremonies to celebrate the opening of new buildings. These don't offer any in-game advantages, but it's a nice photo opportunity.

Isabelle

After the Resident Services Tent is upgraded to a building, you can chat with Isabelle to customize your island's flag, write an original tune for the island, and get advice and updates on your island's star rating. Isabelle will also take over the morning announcements and probably tell you more than you care to know about her TV-viewing habits each day.

Museum

After you donate 5 bugs and/or fish to Tom Nook for him to study, you will unlock the museum, which takes a day to construct and initially appears as a tent. Once it's built, you'll meet its curator, Blathers.

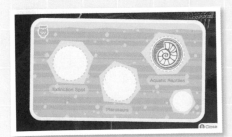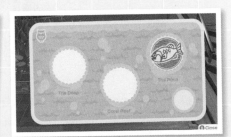

He will accept donations of new bug and fish species, assess fossils, and offer interesting trivia about your donations.

You can enter the museum anytime and enjoy a beautiful set of exhibits that display your hard-won donations.

Upgrading the museum

Once you make 15 donations to Blathers, he will build a proper museum, and once you've donated 60 items, he will open a new wing that accepts art donations.

Fossils

You can find the list of all the fossils that can be donated to Blathers in "Appendix C" at the end of this guide.

Airport/travel agency

The Airport is where you can redeem Nook Miles Tickets to go on Mystery Island Tours, which are random islands with various resources. From here, you can also go on special events-related trips like May Day, and also open up your island to online visitors. Finally, you can buy postcards and send them to your friends on the island or online.

Harv's photo studio

Harv is Animal Crossing's top photographer, and you can visit his island photo studio to take pictures of you and your visiting players with customized backdrops you might otherwise find difficult to buy or craft.

Campsite

The campsite is unlocked after you upgrade the Resident Services Building. Tom Nook will give you the DIY recipe to craft a Campsite Construction Kit and find a spot for it on the island.

Visitors will randomly come to visit the island and camp. If you'd like them to stay, make sure to talk to them a lot and invite them to join you as a permanent resident!

CHAPTER 9

DIY CRAFTING AND RECIPES

DIY crafting requires a workbench and is unlocked almost immediately as there is a workbench in Tom Nook's Resident Services Tent at the start of the game.

At these workbenches, you can craft furniture, tools, and other items if you have the required amount of resources. You can also customize items by buying a Customization Kit from the Nook Stop.

There is an almost unlimited number of recipes to collect in Animal Crossing, and you can acquire them through:

- Purchase
- Gifts from other characters
- Completing special events
- Bottles washed up on shore
- Balloons

62

Key furniture

While most furniture is cosmetic, some furniture actually serves a specific in-game function.

Workbench

These allow you to craft items from DIY recipes. There is always one available in the Resident Services Building, but you might want to add a few more to your house, or near the Nook's Cranny to quickly craft the hot item of the day.

Wardrobe

Pressing "A" near this piece of furniture allows you to access all of your clothing and pick out an outfit.

Mirror

Pressing "A" near the mirror allows you to change your hair color and style. You can buy more options from the Nook Stop.

Toilet

The toilet allows you to negate the effects of eating fruit. This can come in handy if you're afraid that you'll accidentally destroy a rock or tree in your pumped-up state.

CHAPTER 10

DANGERS

You can't really die in Animal Crossing, but there are a couple of ways that you can be hurt.

First, wasp nests can sometimes fall out of trees causing the wasps to sting you. The first sting leaves you with a puffy face but doesn't affect gameplay other than villagers pointing out your haggard appearance. The swelling will go down once you take some medicine (which can be bought at the Nook's Cranny or crafted with a DIY recipe). Or, you can wait a game day and heal naturally. A second bout of stings will reset you back inside your house. Other than this minor inconvenience, you can continue playing as normal.

Second, tarantulas and scorpions can bite you and send you back to your house. Again, this doesn't affect the game much (other than missing out on the opportunity to capture these valuable critters!).

CHAPTER 11

SPECIAL EVENTS

While Animal Crossing is a game packed with fun activities, sometimes it's fun to shake things up with special events. Some events are linked to a specific time of year, while others seem to generate randomly.

Randomly-generated events

These events will eventually occur on certain days, so keep your eye peeled for them!

Meteor shower

During the morning announcements, Isabelle may mention a meteor shower, and island residents might chat about it with you as well. This is great news for you, as meteor showers don't happen often.

In the evening, listen for a tinkling sound, then press the right analog joystick to look up. Make sure that you aren't holding any tools and then press "A" to wish on the star.

If you do this correctly, your character will close their eyes and hold their hands together (the star glows slightly).

Keep looking up after the first star, as several shooting stars often appear in a row.

The next day, walk along the beach, and keep an eye out for yellow rocks near the shoreline, these are called "Star Fragments."

There should be the same number of Star Fragments as wishes you made. These fragments can be used to craft wands (see the Tools section for more details).

While there is no guarantee that you will get a Large Star or Zodiac Fragment (required to craft a wand), as they drop at random whenever you wish on a star—make sure to get in as many wishes as you can.

Wisp

Wisp only comes out at nighttime and randomly appears on certain days, so you just have to keep an eye out for him. Wisp usually appears in forests near the waterline, and you'll probably have to cross a river of some kind to get to him.

By talking to Wisp, you startle him and his spirit explodes into 5 pieces which you must collect from around the island. The pieces look like small wisps of smoke and can be easy to miss, so be thorough. Once found, simply capture them in a bug net.

If you haven't unlocked the pole or ladder yet, you can patiently wait for the wisps to hopefully drift to an accessible area. The quest should continue until morning.

Once you return all of the pieces to Wisp, you are offered two possible rewards: something new or something expensive. Since Bells are fairly easy to earn, and part of the fun of Animal Crossing: New Horizons is customization, we recommend that you choose something new, as you might not get a chance to have it otherwise.

Gulliver

Gulliver can always be found on the beach and can't seem to keep his Communicator in one piece. If you help him find the 5 parts for his Communicator that are buried in the sand (sand blowing out of holes) you will receive exclusive furniture. Helping Gulliver 30 times unlocks the Golden Shovel.

Mystery Island Tours

If you want a little excitement, you can purchase a Nook Miles Ticket at the Resident Services Tent or the shopping app on your phone to buy a ticket to another island for 2,000 Nook Miles. These islands are randomly assigned but follow specific designs. The more you travel, the more opportunities you have to stumble upon special islands that have bamboo trees or are even infested with valuable tarantulas!

You might also run into a character on one of these trips that you can invite to come live on your island.

Time-locked events

There are many events, and some are region specific. For the purpose of this guide, we will focus on events that occur in North America. Time-locked events are always being added, so make sure that you listen to Isabelle's morning announcements to hear what's coming up.

Snowboy

Snowboy is a winter character that you can build around mid-December. You can only make snowballs if your island is covered in snow.

Roll up a snowball by avoiding any trees and water, which will destroy them. If your snowball is destroyed, entering a building will cause a new one to appear.

It's easy to make a Snowboy, but if you put in the extra effort, you can make a Perfect Snowboy that will produce a Large Snowflake for 3 days before he melts. Large Snowflakes can be used to craft ice-themed DIY items.

To make a Perfect Snowboy, your base snowball should be the maximum size. You'll know you've reached the maximum size when your character slows down while rolling the snowball. If you make the snowball too big, you can always start over.

The second snowball should be about 10% smaller than the body, but not the same size. Snowboy will let you know if you made him perfectly.

If you made an imperfect Snowboy, you can either reset your game and try again before it autosaves or try again the next day. You can only build one Snowboy a day, but you can have more than one on your island at a time!

Bug Off

The Bug Off is hosted by Flick and occurs every 3rd Saturday during the summer from 5 AM to 6 PM. The entry fee is 500 Bells, but the first time is free.

The Bug Off is essentially a time trial where you have 3 minutes to catch as many bugs as you can. If you focus, you'll easily make back your entry fee by selling your bugs to Flick. There is no limit on how many times you can play, so feel free to participate multiple times.

If you catch more than 3 bugs, you will score bonus points, which you can spend on rewards and include some items.

Bug-Off Event Rewards

All items cost 10 points. The order of items may be random:

- Artisanal Bug Cage
- Bug Aloha Shirt
- Bug Cage
- Bug Wand
- Butterfly Backpack
- Butterfly Wall

- Ladybug Rug
- Ladybug Umbrella
- Spider Doorplate
- Termite Mound
- Toy Centipede
- Toy Cockroach

The item you might want to prioritize is the Bug Wand, which allows you to change outfits instantly. Other types of wands require Star Fragments to craft and are much harder to acquire (see the Tools section for more information on wands).

Fishing tournament

Fishing tournaments are held by C.J. on the 2nd Saturday of every month. These are separate from the fishing challenges he offers when he appears on other days.

The Fishing Tournament is similar to the Bug Off, in that C.J. gives you 3 minutes to catch as many fish as possible. Any fish caught during this time are sent to C.J.'s cooler box, so even if your inventory is full you won't have to waste time swapping out items.

Some tips for a successful round of fishing include:

- Having a second fishing rod ready in case your current one breaks
- Having at least 10 bags of bait ready

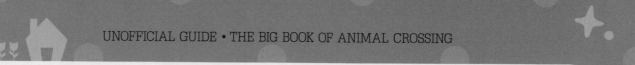

- Fishing in the sea where the fish are bigger
- Having your fishing rod already equipped when you talk to C.J. so that you don't waste any time getting your line in the water

Depending on how many fish you catch, you will earn points that you can cash in by talking to C.J. afterwards. If you catch more than 3 fish within the 3-minute time period, you automatically get 2 extra bonus points.

You can continue entering the Fishing Tournament all day to build up points and rack up fish to sell to C.J. later (or keep for yourself).

If you earn 100, 200, or 300 points, you will also be awarded either a bronze, silver, or gold trophy, respectively. Not bad for a day's fishin'!

Fishing Tournament Rewards List

Here are all of the prizes that you can win on the Fishing Tournament:

- Tackle Bag
- Fish Umbrella
- Fish-Drying Rack
- Fish Print
- Fresh Cooler
- Fish Rug
- Fish Doorplate

- Fish-Print Tee
- Fish Wand
- Marine Pop Wall
- Fishing-Rod Stand
- Anchor Statue
- Fish Pochette

Special holidays

Always be sure to check out your island on special holidays or days you might find marked on a calendar, such as Easter, Christmas, Valentine's Day, St. Patrick's Day, Labor Day, Halloween, New Year's Day, Groundhog Day, and even your birthday! The game developers are always adding in new special days and might have something fun prepared for you.

CHAPTER 12

ISLAND RESIDENTS

Filbert

Your island can house a maximum of 10 villagers, and you'll need a healthy population if you want to earn a 5-star rating.

Residents are automatically added during the game's progression, but you can speed up the process by inviting characters that you meet on Mystery Island Tours to join you. Of course, you need to already have a dwelling for them to move into, so that means helping Tom Nook expand the island infrastructure.

Residents wander around and do their own thing, but there are a few ways you can interact with them:

- Chatting with them treats you to some fun dialogue, and sometimes they give you random gifts
- Giving them a gift often causes them to reciprocate
- If a resident has a problem, such as becoming sick or losing an item, you are given a gift if you help them by bringing medicine or returning their belonging

- Residents will randomly teach you how to emote, which is useful for playing with other human players online. You can access this menu by holding down the right shoulder button and picking an emotion from the radial menu. There are 44 emotions to collect!

- Visiting them at home might find them hard at work on a DIY recipe. You can offer to help them and learn a new DIY recipe

Removing villagers

While most villagers in Animal Crossing are adorable, you might find someone who has moved in to be annoying or simply want to try meeting someone new.

You might be tempted to complain about a villager to Isabelle, if for example they are wearing an outfit that you don't like or they learn a weird phrase from a visiting player. However, this only resets your villager back to their base mode.

A better strategy is to ignore the villager you wish would leave. Do not interact with them at all and continue talking to the other villagers. If you'd like, you can even build a fence around their house so that they're unable to even roam the island.

Check in on the villager over the next couple of days and see if they have a thought bubble over their head or run toward you and shout your name. It is possible, they will confess they are thinking of leaving, at which point you can heartily encourage this decision.

Adding specific villagers

While most villagers appear randomly, if you have the amiibo figurine of a villager you'd like to have join your island, you can summon them to your campsite by chatting with Isabelle in the Resident Services Building.

While there, they will covet a specific DIY recipe which you should craft for them. Keep talking to them and giving them presents for at least 3 days.

If there is an empty dwelling for them to occupy, follow the discussion prompts to encourage them to move in.

Bonus: if you already have 10 villagers, the incoming character will mention that they heard someone was thinking of moving out. Feel free to drop the name of a villager you wish would leave, and they will be replaced by your new friend.

CHAPTER 13

ADVANCED TIPS

Making big money fast

Considering Animal Crossing: New Horizons doesn't place much emphasis on goals, you have to decide what's most important to you. Is it building up the perfect crash pad? Lining the perimeter of your island with rare plants? Giving extravagant gifts to your fellow residents? All of these involve Bells, the major currency in the game.

With that in mind, beware of some of the tips in this section, because when Bells are no object, you'll be depriving yourself of the soothing joy of many of the game's activities. That being said, let's get rich!

Smart selling

While there are limits on the items you can sell early on in the game, over time, some money-making activities are more worth your time than others.

Tarantulas

Rare fish may fetch high prices, but tarantulas spawn fairly often at night. When you see one, drop everything to catch it—each one sells for 8,000 Bells. See the Tools section for tips on how to catch this dangerous creature with a net.

Money trees

When you find a glowing spot on the ground and dig it up, you will be awarded a nice chunk of Bells. But don't go for the quick win, this is your opportunity to grow a money tree! Yes, in Animal Crossing, money does grow on trees!

Basically, if you bury Bells in the glowing hole, a tree will sprout. Over time it will grow into a money tree, which will grow bags of Bells like fruit that you can harvest—but only once.

The number of Bells that you bury will affect the money tree's harvest yield. For example, if you bury 1,000 Bells, you'll be treated to a harvest of 3,000 Bells. Money is generally tripled up to 10,000 Bells so it is worth making the initial investment. However, if you bury more than that, you are not guaranteed triple.

To do this, simply stand next to the glowing hole and highlight the Bells in your inventory. If you press "A" while on it, you are given the option to transfer Bells into your inventory. Pick 10,000, then press "A" on the bag of Bells in your inventory while your shovel is equipped and then select "Bury in the ground."

Exotic fruit from other islands

While the fruit native to your island fetches a decent price, exotic fruit sells for even more. Whenever you are traveling (to a friend's island online or on a Mystery Island Tour), make sure to collect not only fruit from these places but fruit trees as well. As discussed earlier, a tree can be uprooted using a shovel if you first eat fruit to supercharge your energy.

You can then plant these trees on your own island and have a renewable source of high-value fruit to sell.

Fossils

Once you've consistently donated fossils to the museum for a while, Blathers will more frequently inform you that an assessed fossil is already part of the collection. These fossils fetch a good price at the Nook's Cranny, so make sure that you search and dig up the 4 fossils that spawn every day on your island.

The Stalk Market

Get into the habit of purchasing as many turnips as you can afford on Sundays, then check back in at the Nook's Cranny frequently over the next week for the going turnip rates. Much like the real-life stock market, even a profit of 10 Bells per turnip is impressive when you've invested 10,000 Bells. Just remember that you can't keep turnips in storage, and make sure that you sell them before they spoil, which takes about a week after you buy them.

The Money Rock

Every day one of the rocks on your island will be designated a Money Rock, and instead of minerals, it will produce Bells. If you use the rock mining strategy outlined in the Shovel Tool section, you can maximize your harvest to 8.

Hot items

Once the Nook's Cranny is upgraded to its own store, each day it will post a hot item, which is something you can sell for approximately double the regular price. It's often something you can easily craft on a DIY workbench, so that's pure profit.

Load up on Mystery Island Tours

For the cost of 2,000 Nook Miles, you can visit a random island. Make sure that your inventory space is upgraded to the maximum (see the Inventory section on how to do this), then put everything but your tools in storage, and go load up. By taking advantage of the island's rocks, fruits, shells, and other resources, you'll easily earn a hefty return on your investment in a ticket.

Also, if you're lucky enough to find the fairly rare Tarantula Island, don't freak out! It's a spooky place, but by using some simple strategies, you can harvest a ton of Tarantulas and sell them back on your island for big profit.

Time traveling

Now for the dark magic of Animal Crossing. Once again, fair warning that using this technique will destroy a lot of the enjoyment that the game provides.

It is possible to time travel by changing the date and time on your Nintendo Switch. Since the game relies on the system clock to operate its time-gating system, this will affect your island in several ways. There are a few ways this shady technique can be advantageous:

- Generating a ton of Bells and resources
- Switching between day or night at your leisure to target specific bugs and fish or trigger time-related special events
- Switching dates to catch missed date-specific special events
- Reliving missed time-locked events connected to specific dates like Bunny Day
- Jumping to specific seasons to catch specific bugs and fish
- Speeding up time-locked events, such as constructing buildings

However, there are a few downsides to time traveling, including:

- Your island may become overgrown with weeds
- Your flowers may die
- You may miss out on a rare item for sale in the store
- Villagers may move out
- Your mailbox may become full and unable to receive new messages until cleaned out
- Cockroaches may infest your house
- Your turnips will rot
- Your player's appearance will become ragged
- Nintendo and the Animal Crossing community look down on and discourage this practice

That being said, none of these consequences are devastating. Cockroaches are easily stomped out, weeds can be pulled, and new villagers can once again be found. The real risk is ruining your enjoyment of the game by making things too easy.

How to time travel

- Navigate to the "System Settings" on your console
- Select "System"
- Select "Date and Time"
- Disable the feature "Synchronize Clock via Internet"
- Select the new time zone, date, and time you'd like to play in

Animal Crossing: New Horizons has an auto-save feature, so once you play for a few minutes after time traveling, you won't be able to reload an old saved game to take back what you've done.

Earning Bells through time travel

If you're still keen on time travel, here are some strategies for earning Bells.

Savings account

The easiest way to rack up Bells with time travel is to travel forward through time with money in your savings account at the ABM. Savings accounts rack up interest over time, so jumping a couple of years in the future will max out the interest at 99,000 Bells.

The Stalk Market

This requires visiting a friend's island. Simply ask them to let you know when their island is selling turnips at a high price. As mentioned earlier, anything over 200 Bells is pretty good, but this strategy works best when the prices are a bit higher, between 300 and 400 Bells.

Simply change your system clock to Sunday between 5 AM and noon, and buy as many turnips from Daisy Mae as you can afford. Then, (without changing your clock back to the true date and time as this may spoil your turnips) visit your friend's island and sell the turnips. Depending on the size of your inventory and turnip prices, you can make as much as 2 million Bells in one trip!

Once your turnips are sold, return your system clock to its proper date and enjoy your profit!

This strategy is a little bit safer than the Savings Account strategy because it only involves changing the time and date by less than 7 days to get to the closest Sunday. While it does require an accomplice, you can sweeten the deal for your friend by offering them a cut of your Bells for their time.

Daily tasks you should complete every day

If you are short on time to play, here is a handy list of activities you can complete to make sure you're earning as many Bells as you can every day in under 30 minutes.

Log in to the Nook Stop

You earn Nook Miles every day just by using the machine in Tom Nook's shop. The bonus starts at 50, but if you get a string of consecutive login days going, you will eventually earn 300 Nook Miles just for logging in. That's a pretty good deal!

Dig up new fossils

While you tour your island, watch out for patches of ground that appear to have a dark star shape on them. These indicate buried fossils which re-spawn every day, and there are always 4-5 to find. These fossils can be assessed at the museum and sold for Bells. If you're having trouble finding all of the fossils, check behind bushes and furniture—they won't spawn behind trees.

Mine rocks

Rocks can only be mined once per day, so it's worth hitting them all up to get valuable iron and gold nuggets. There is also a Money Rock which gives out Bells and bags of Bells. If you move fast enough (see the Shovel section for tips on how to maximize your rock harvests), you can collect up to 16,400 Bells!

Search for washed-up bottles

There is usually a new message in a bottle washed up somewhere on the beach every day. These bottles are a source of potential new DIY recipes.

Keep an eye out for balloons

Know that any play session over 5 minutes means that a balloon has spawned somewhere over the sea and is floating toward your island. Keep an eye out for balloons, as they can drop valuable Bells or even a rare DIY recipe.

Interact with visitors and island residents

Interacting with other characters on the island can earn you Nook Challenge points as well as trigger special events. Your neighbors might also give you a gift, especially if you offer them a gift first.

Complete Nook Bonus tasks

At any given time, there are 5 bonus tasks listed on your phone. These are randomly generated and offer various score multipliers reaching as high as 5 times the Nook Miles. Get in the habit of cashing in these tasks as soon as they are complete because they will refresh with new tasks that you might perform as a regular part of your day—you might as well get bonuses for them.

5-star island rating

One of the major long-term goals of Animal Crossing: New Horizons is to achieve the coveted 5-star rating for your island. Aside from bragging rights in the Animal Crossing community, this rating unlocks the Golden Watering Can, and at 3 stars, you will unlock the awesome character K.K. Slider.

So how do you achieve a 5-star rating? There are several steps. It is the hardest challenge in the game after all!

Unlocking island evaluations

As you unlock major buildings and characters in the game, you might not even be aware that your island is up for evaluation. So how do you get to that stage?

- Upgrade the Resident Services Tent to a building, build the museum and the Nook's Cranny, build your first bridge, and help with site picking and furnishings for three new homes in addition to your first two neighbors. All of these projects are triggered by chatting with Tom Nook and take time to complete.
- Build a campground to help Tom Nook attract more residents to the island. When someone comes to stay at the campsite, invite them to live on your island.

- After you pick a spot for the incoming villager, talk to Tom Nook, who will outline his plan to improve your island's star rating.
- At this point, Isabelle will be your point of contact for island rating issues and will offer her advice.

Achieving a better island rating

Isabelle will let you know some of the more important features for improving your rating. These include:

- Trees
- Fencing
- Absence of garbage and weeds
- Outdoor furniture (such as benches or campfires) for residents to enjoy
- Close to the maximum of 10 villagers living on the island
- Flowers

These items are not an exact science. For example, there is no magic number of flowers or trees to plant. However, Isabelle will give you tips on what aspects of the above list you should be focusing on.

Specific tips

Consider using fencing around your gardens. This will count toward the fencing component of your rating and allow you to create hybrid flowers using the 5x5 square gardening strategy (outlined in the Resources section above) and avoid any unwanted cross-pollination.

Add fencing to your fellow residents' yards and treat each property with the same loving care that you spent on your own house—add gardens and outdoor furniture like barbecues and hammocks.

Don't be afraid to cash in your hard-earned Nook Miles on big, expensive outdoor items that Tom Nook sells, like the lighthouse.

While trees are important, the random spacing of them in the game is inefficient. Consider cutting down some trees and organizing them a little bit better so that you can clear room for dedicated flower gardens and outdoor furniture.

You can even place cool furniture on rocky areas. Why not install a bath overlooking the sea?

Terraform your island to fill in some of the water areas to free up valuable land for outdoor furniture.

Instead of selling fossils, hang onto them until you have a full set. Some of the dinosaur skeletons make epic statues for your island residents to enjoy.

Maximize your waterfront property by decorating your beaches with the appropriate items.

Visit other players' islands and see if they will gift you any unique items that you can add to your collection.

Your rewards

A 5-star rating not only unlocks the Golden Watering Can but a new type of flower called Lily of the Valley, which can be found near cliffs. It will only grow on islands with a 5-star rating, so if your rating slips, you won't be able to buy or breed new ones.

Linking with Animal Crossing: Pocket Camp

Link two accounts to unlock a Special Orders Ticket—a redeemable code that unlocks unique items. You will also receive 50 Leaf Tickets in Pocket Camp along with crossover items like Tom Nook's office table.

CHAPTER 14

HAPPY TRAVELS

Now that you have a full understanding of Animal Crossing:
New Horizons, you will be able to maximize
the fun and pleasure that this rich and wonderful
game has to offer. Have fun, and remember...

It's not the destination that matters, it's the journey!

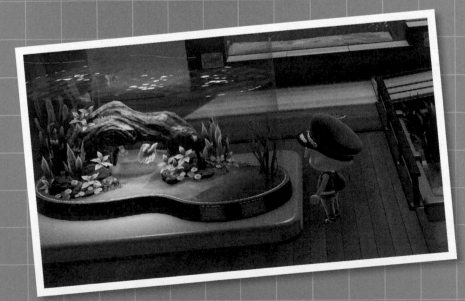

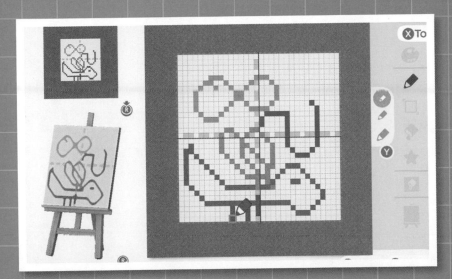

Appendix A: Insects

	Jan	Feb	Mar	Apr	May	June	July	Aug	Sept	Oct	Nov	Dec
FLYING												
Common Butterfly	x	x	x	x	x	x			x	x	x	x
Yellow Butterfly			x	x	x				x	x		
Tiger Butterfly			x	x	x	x	x	x	x			
Peacock Butterfly			x	x	x	x						
Common Bluebottle				x	x	x	x	x				
Paper Kite Butterfly	x	x	x	x	x	x	x	x	x	x	x	x
Great Purple Emperor					x	x	x	x				
Monarch Butterfly									x	x	x	
Emperor Butterfly	x	x	x			x	x	x	x			x
Agrias Butterfly				x	x	x	x	x	x			
Rajah Brooke's Birdwing	x	x		x	x	x	x	x	x			x
Queen Alexandra's Birdwing					x	x	x	x	x			
Banded Dragonfly					x	x	x	x	x	x		
Mosquito						x	x	x	x			
Firefly (near rivers)						x						
PONDS												
Pondskater				x	x	x	x	x	x			
Diving Beetle				x	x	x	x	x	x			
Giant Water Bug				x	x	x	x	x	x			
FLOWERS												
Madagascan Sunset Moth				x	x	x	x	x	x			
Mantis			x	x	x	x	x	x	x	x	x	
Orchid Mantis			x	x	x	x	x	x	x	x	x	
Honeybee			x	x	x	x	x					
Stinkbug			x	x	x	x	x	x	x	x		
Man-Faced Stink Bug			x	x	x	x	x	x	x	x		
Ladybug			x	x	x	x				x		
PALM TREES												
Blue Weevil Beetle							x	x				
Goliath Beetle						x	x	x	x			
Cyclommatus Stag							x	x				
Golden Stag							x	x				
Giraffe Stag							x	x				
Horned Atlas							x	x				
Horned Elephant							x	x				
Horned Hercules							x	x				

	Jan	Feb	Mar	Apr	May	June	July	Aug	Sept	Oct	Nov	Dec
GROUND												
Long Locust				x	x	x	x	x	x	x	x	
Migratory Locust								x	x	x	x	
Rice Grasshopper								x	x	x	x	
Grasshopper							x	x	x			
Cricket								x	x	x		
Bell Cricket								x	x			
Red Dragonfly								x	x			
Darner Dragonfly				x	x	x	x	x	x	x		
Damselfly	x	x									x	x
Tiger Beetle		x	x	x	x	x	x	x	x	x		
Tarantula	x	x	x	x							x	x
Scorpion					x	x	x	x	x	x		
BEACHES												
Wharf Roach	x	x	x	x	x	x	x	x	x	x	x	x
Hermit Crab	x	x	x	x	x	x	x	x	x	x	x	x
TREES												
Jewel Beetle				x	x	x	x	x				
Violin Beetle				x	x				x	x	x	
Citrus Long-Horned Beetle	x	x	x	x	x	x	x	x	x	x	x	x
Rosalia Batesi Beetle					x	x	x	x	x			
Atlas Moth				x	x	x	x	x	x			
Brown Cicada							x	x				
Robust Cicada							x	x				
Giant Cicada							x	x				
Walker Cicada								x	x			
Evening Cicada							x	x				
Cicada Shell							x	x				
Earth-Boring Dung Beetle							x	x	x			
Drone Beetle						x	x	x				
Miyama Stag							x	x				
Horned Dynastid							x	x				
Scarab Beetle							x	x				
Saw Stag							x	x				
Giant Stag							x	x				
Rainbow Stag						x	x	x	x			
Walking Stick							x	x	x	x	x	
MISCELLANEOUS												
Ant *On turnips*	x	x	x	x	x	x	x	x	x	x	x	x
Flea *On villagers*				x	x	x	x	x	x	x	x	
Pill Bug *Rocks when hit with a shovel*	x	x	x	x	x	x			x	x	x	x
Centipede *Rocks when hit with a shovel*	x	x	x	x	x	x			x	x	x	x
Wasp (Bee) *Trees when shaken*	x	x	x	x	x	x	x	x	x	x	x	x
Bagworm *Trees when shaken*	x	x	x	x	x	x	x	x	x	x	x	x

	Jan	Feb	Mar	Apr	May	June	July	Aug	Sept	Oct	Nov	Dec
Spider *Trees when shaken*	x	x	x	x	x	x	x	x	x	x	x	x
Walking Leaf *Under trees*							x	x	x			
Mole Cricket *Underground*	x	x	x	x	x						x	x
Moth *Near outside lights*	x	x	x	x	x	x	x	x	x	x	x	x
Dung Beetle *Near snowballs*	x	x										x
Snail *On rocks in the rain*	x	x	x	x	x	x	x	x	x	x	x	x
Fly *On spoiled turnips and trash*	x	x	x	x	x	x	x	x	x	x	x	x

Appendix B: Fishes

	Jan	Feb	Mar	Apr	May	June	July	Aug	Sept	Oct	Nov	Dec
CLIFFTOP												
Cherry Salmon			x	x	x	x			x	x	x	
Char			x	x	x	x			x	x	x	
Golden Trout			x	x	x				x	x	x	
Stringfish	x	x	x									x
PIER												
Tuna	x	x	x	x							x	x
Blue Marlin	x	x	x	x			x	x	x		x	x
Giant Trevally					x	x	x	x	x	x		
Mahi-Mahi					x	x	x	x	x	x		
POND												
Carp	x	x	x	x	x	x	x	x	x	x	x	x
Koi	x	x	x	x	x	x	x	x	x	x	x	x
Goldfish	x	x	x	x	x	x	x	x	x	x	x	x
Pop-Eyed Goldfish	x	x	x	x	x	x	x	x	x	x	x	x
Ranchu Goldfish	x	x	x	x	x	x	x	x	x	x	x	x
Killifish				x	x	x	x	x				
Crawfish				x	x	x	x	x	x			
Tadpole			x	x	x	x	x					
Frog					x	x	x	x				
Catfish					x	x	x	x	x	x		
Giant Snakehead						x	x	x				
Gar						x	x	x	x			
RIVER												
Bitterling	x	x	x								x	x
Pale Chub	x	x	x	x	x	x	x	x	x	x	x	x
Crucian Carp	x	x	x	x	x	x	x	x	x	x	x	x
Dace	x	x	x	x	x	x	x	x	x	x	x	x
Soft-Shelled Turtle								x	x			
Snapping Turtle				x	x	x	x	x	x	x		
Freshwater Goby	x	x	x	x	x	x	x	x	x	x	x	x
Loach			x	x	x							
Bluegill	x	x	x	x	x		x	x	x	x	x	x
Yellow Perch	x	x	x							x	x	x
Black Bass	x	x	x	x	x	x	x	x	x	x	x	x
Tilapia						x	x	x	x	x		
Pike									x	x	x	x
Pond Smelt	x	x										x
Sweetfish							x	x	x			
Mitten Crab									x	x	x	
Guppy				x	x	x	x	x	x	x	x	
Nibble Fish				x	x	x	x	x	x			
Angelfish				x	x	x	x	x	x	x		
Betta				x	x	x	x	x	x	x		
Neon Tetra				x	x	x	x	x	x	x	x	
Rainbowfish					x	x	x	x	x	x		
Piranha						x	x	x	x			
Arowana						x	x	x	x			

	Jan	Feb	Mar	Apr	May	June	July	Aug	Sept	Oct	Nov	Dec
Dorado						x	x	x	x			
Arapaima						x	x	x	x			
Saddled Bichir						x	x	x	x			
Salmon									x			
King Salmon									x			
Sturgeon	x	x	x						x	x	x	x
SEA												
Sea Butterfly	x	x	x									x
Seahorse				x	x	x	x	x	x	x	x	
Clownfish				x	x	x	x	x	x			
Surgeonfish				x	x	x	x	x	x			
Butterfly Fish				x	x	x	x	x	x			
Napoleon fish							x	x				
Zebra Turkeyfish				x	x	x	x	x	x	x	x	
Blowfish	x	x									x	x
Puffer Fish							x	x	x			
Anchovy	x	x	x	x	x	x	x	x	x	x	x	x
Horse Mackerel	x	x	x	x	x	x	x	x	x	x	x	x
Barred Knifejaw			x	x	x	x	x	x	x	x	x	
Sea Bass	x	x	x	x	x	x	x	x	x	x	x	x
Red Snapper	x	x	x	x	x	x	x	x	x	x	x	x
Dab	x	x	x	x						x	x	x
Olive Flounder	x	x	x	x	x	x	x	x	x	x	x	x
Squid	x	x	x	x	x	x	x	x				x
Moray Eel								x	x	x		
Ribbon Eel						x	x	x	x	x		
Ocean Sunfish							x	x	x			
Ray								x	x	x	x	
Saw Shark						x	x	x	x			
Hammerhead Shark						x	x	x	x			
Great White Shark						x	x	x	x			
Whale Shark						x	x	x	x			
Suckerfish						x	x	x	x			
Football Fish	x	x	x								x	x
Oarfish	x	x	x	x	x							x
Barreleye	x	x	x	x	x	x	x	x	x	x	x	x
Coelacanth (Rainy days only)	x	x	x	x	x	x	x	x	x	x	x	x

Appendix C: Fossils

SET	PART
SELL PRICE: 1,000+	
Dinosaur Track	Individual
Juramaia	Individual
Shark Tooth Pattern	Individual
Ammonite	Individual
Australopithecus	Individual
Coprolite	Individual
Amber	Individual
Archaeopteryx	Individual
Trilobite	Individual
Myllokunmingia	Individual
SELL PRICE: 2,000+	
Acanthostega	Individual
Anomalocaris	Individual
Eusthenopteron	Individual
Ophthalmosaurus	Opthalmo Torso
Ophthalmosaurus	Opthalmo Skull
Sabertooth Tiger	Sabertooth Tail
Sabertooth Tiger	Sabertooth Skull
Spinosaurus	Spino Tail
Ankylosaurus	Ankylo Tail
Deinonychus	Deinony Tail
Mammoth	Mammoth Torso
Parasaurolophus	Parasaur Tail
SELL PRICE: 3,000+	
Ankylosaurus	Ankylo Torso
Ankylosaurus	Ankylo Skull
Deinonychus	Deinony Torso
Iguanodon	Iguanodon Tail
Iguanodon	Iguanodon Torso
Mammoth	Mammoth Skull
Megacerops	Megacro Tail
Megacerops	Megacero Torso
Parasaurolophus	Parasaur Torso
Parasaurolophus	Parasaur Skull
Spinosaurus	Spino Torso
Archelon	Archelon Tail
Dunkleosteus	Individual
Pachycephalosaurus	Pachy Tail

SET	PART
SELL PRICE: 4,000+	
Archelon	Archelon Skull
Diplodocus	Diplo Chest
Diplodocus	Diplo Tail Tip
Diplodocus	Diplo Pelvis
Iguanodon	Iguanodon Skull
Megaloceros	Megalo Left Side
Pachycephalosaurus	Pachy Skull
Plesiosaurus	Plesio Skull
Plesiosaurus	Plesio Torso
Plesiosaurus	Plesio Tail
Pteranodon	Ptera Body
Pteranodon	Right Ptera Wing
Pteranodon	Left Ptera Wing
Spinosaurus	Spino Skull
Stegosaurus	Stego Tail
Stegosaurus	Stego Torso
Megacerops	Megacro Skull
Quetzalcoatlus	Quetzal Torso
Triceratops	Tricera Tail
SELL PRICE: 5,000+	
Brachiosaurus	Brachio Pelvis
Brachiosaurus	Brachio Chest
Brachiosaurus	Brachio Tail
Dimetrodon	Dimetrodon Torso
Dimetrodon	Dimetrodon Skull
Diplodocus	Diplo Skull
Diplodocus	Diplo Neck
Diplodocus	Diplo Tail
Quetzalcoatlus	Right Quetzal Wing
Quetzalcoatlus	Quetzal Left Wing
Stegosaurus	Stego Skull
Tyrannosaurus Rex	T. Rex Tail
Tyrannosaurus Rex	T. Rex Torso
Megaloceros	Megalo Right Side
Triceratops	Tricera Torso
SELL PRICE: 6,000+	
Brachiosaurus	Brachio Skull
Triceratops	Tricera Skull
Tyrannosaurus Rex	T. Rex Skull